OLIVER!
and His Friends

and His Friends

by Mary Hastings

Adapted from the screenplay based on Lionel Bart's "Oliver!"
freely adapted from Charles Dickens' "Oliver Twist"

Illustrated with photographs from the motion picture

 Random House • New York

Outside the workhouse, lightning flickered across a sign on the big iron gate. HOME FOR PAUPERS AND ORPHANS, it read. Rain splattered down, puddling the cobblestone courtyard, and thunder roared. Inside, in a windowless room, a baby gasped and bellowed out the first sounds of its new life.

Fat Widow Corney sighed impatiently, waiting for the doctor to speak.

"Well, Doctor?" she whined at last. "What *is* it?"

The doctor glared at the widow with disgust. Clearly he hated the workhouse, and he was in a hurry to leave now that his work was done.

"It's a boy," he said. "But the mother, poor soul, is dead."

He snapped his bag shut and left.

As soon as the doctor had gone, Widow Corney began searching through the young mother's few belongings. She grumbled when she found nothing there of value. Then, picking up the baby, she bustled out of the room and headed down the hall to another room marked ORPHAN INFANTS. This room was windowless like the first. It was furnished

3

with small, rough, wooden boxes which served as cradles for several tiny babies. Into such a box Widow Corney put the newborn infant before going off to her own comfortable bed.

The workhouse, with its gaunt old folks and ragamuffin children, did not pay any attention to the new arrival. It was supposed to be a place of charity, but it was really a house of work. Here children too young and men and women too old labored without pay. The rich men in town bragged about their kindness in taking care of the shiftless poor. But they didn't do anything except to make sure that no money came out of their own pockets.

Besides Widow Corney there was only one other paid official at the workhouse. He was Mr. Bumble, a petty official of the town with no specific job to do. For Mr. Bumble the workhouse provided a kind of refuge. A fat, unpleasant man, he was disliked throughout the town. So he enjoyed visiting the workhouse, where the children and old people were forced to treat him with respect. He was also fond of the Widow Corney; and the widow repaid his admiration by sharing her work with him.

So it was that the job of naming the boy, born and orphaned that rainy night, was given to Mr. Bumble. The fat man called him Oliver Twist.

When Oliver Twist grew too big for his box cradle, he was moved into a

dormitory with the other boys. There he was given a hard plank bed to sleep on. As soon as this happened, Oliver was considered old enough to work at the treadmill. In fact, he practically learned to walk at the treadmill. The work was hard and boring, but most of the boys labored obediently. Scant food, hard work, little sleep, and regular beatings from Mr. Bumble kept the children from boyish rebellion.

But Oliver Twist would not have rebelled even if he could have—it wasn't in his nature. He worked when he had to, ate what little he was given, and slept when he could. He was always tired, but

he did not mind his life. To him the workhouse was more than a home—it was his whole world. He knew no other. A kind boy, he was well liked by the few who knew him. But for the most part his presence at the workhouse was scarcely noticed. Only troublesome boys were noticed, and Oliver Twist was no trouble at all.

But the hunger was difficult. And it was that never-ending gnawing in the stomach that led to trouble.

A day was set aside each month for the wealthy men of the town to make a charity call on the workhouse. On that day smells of glorious food drifted from

the governors' dining room, making the boys sniff and their stomachs rumble. It was hard to bear, for it stirred the boys' imaginations with dreams of a better life. On one such day it was the misfortune of Oliver Twist to be in the wrong place at the wrong time.

Lunch was late and for once the boys had a moment between working and eating to sniff at the governors' window and to talk among themselves. In a corner of the yard, Oliver and a few other boys huddled together, whispering.

Oliver watched with interest as an older boy stooped down and gathered up a handful of straws. The boy turned his back and broke the straws into different lengths. Then he turned around, clutching the straws in one hand so that only one end of each straw was visible. Each boy—including Oliver—solemnly chose a straw. Then, in great suspense, they compared lengths.

"Ha! Ha! Oliver," cried one with relief. "You've got the short one. You have to ask."

6

Oliver fidgeted with his straw. He wished with all his heart that he had not chosen to enter the game.

"Must I?" he pleaded. "I'm not hungry. Really I'm not."

"If you don't we'll eat your gruel," said the others. "We want more. And if you don't get it for us we'll eat yours."

The boys didn't mean any harm. They had drawn straws fairly and Oliver had drawn the short one. They were just hungry. And so was Oliver Twist.

"All right," he said, "I'll do it."

"Hurray!" cheered the boys. "Hurray for Oliver Twist!"

Just then the lunch bell rang and Mr. Bumble appeared.

"Silence!" he shouted. "Step lively now—and no talking."

The barefoot boys shuffled silently

into line and marched into the work-house. Several of the governors stepped into the hall to watch them pass. Bumble smiled, and patted a few of the boys on the head in a sudden display of affection.

As soon as Mr. Bumble had left the eating hall, excitement filled the room. Word of what Oliver was about to do spread quickly. As they gulped down their gruel, the boys talked and sang of glorious food. Then Mr. Bumble returned with the Widow Corney.

"Come on, Oliver," whispered a boy as the stout couple strode to the front of the room.

After much nudging and whispering, Oliver stood up. Carrying his wooden bowl and spoon before him, he marched boldly up to Mr. Bumble.

9

"Please, sir," he said in a small, clear voice. "I want some more."

"M-o-o-o-o-re?" roared Mr. Bumble.

His face turned crimson, his arms flew up in the air, and he took a step toward Oliver. Never before had a workhouse boy dared to ask for more.

Trembling with fear, Oliver backed a few steps, spun around, and fled. Over tables and under benches he scrambled as Bumble and several old men chased him. The other boys, wanting to appear innocent, rose from their benches and ran after Oliver, too.

"Catch him!" bellowed Bumble.

"Hold him!" screeched the Widow.

Oliver leaped from a table to a high window sill. But the window was barred. He jumped to the floor and rushed up the stairs toward the door. There two

old men grabbed him and held him to the floor. The room became silent.

"Got him!" Bumble chuckled as he puffed up the stairs. "So it's more you want, is it? Then more you shall have—more cockroaches to eat, more beatings to keep you warm, and much more trouble than you bargained for."

He took Oliver firmly by the ear and dragged him down the hall to the governors' dining room. Oliver had never seen such food as was spread before the governors. Turkey, potatoes, pie and fine wine were spread out on a fancy white tablecloth. The fat men laughed and burped luxuriously. They were obviously not thinking about works of charity.

Mr. Bumble explained breathlessly what Oliver had done.

"Such greed!" exclaimed a man with gravy on his shirt.

"We've spoiled him," said a fat man, his mouth full.

"Sell the brat," said another, and the rest of the men heartily agreed.

12

Oliver's departure from the workhouse was prompt and of little importance. One boy more or less did not matter. So when Mr. Bumble led him out the door that day there were no good-bys. Nobody even noticed.

From Oliver's standpoint, however, the day was remarkable in several ways. In the first place, he was wearing his first pair of shoes. These did not please him for he had no socks; and the shoes, being several sizes too large, made his feet and ankles raw. Still, he had to admit that it was better than walking barefoot in the snow.

The second thing which impressed him was the gate. Never before in the entire nine years of his life had Oliver Twist set foot outside the huge iron gate. Now, as it closed behind him, Oliver looked back and suddenly wondered whether the gate was meant to keep people in or out. Were the friends he left behind prisoners in the workhouse and was he, Oliver Twist, now free? Or was it the other way around? He did not know. It was simply amazing to be on the other side of that gate.

The fact that he was to be sold did not disturb Oliver in the least. His experience at the workhouse had given him no self-respect, so being sold did not seem to be a terrible thing. He even half hoped that the transaction would somehow put him in better circumstances. But with only a bit of burlap over his shirtsleeves for warmth, Oliver was soon too cold to keep his mind on such speculations. Carrying his small bundle of belongings, he trudged silently after Mr. Bumble.

It was snowing hard when the two reached the Dunstable Market. Footsore and shivering, Oliver took little notice of the new sights around him. He simply followed the heavy guiding hand of Mr. Bumble, trying to look healthy and happy—as the fat man had ordered.

Here and there were signs that said APPRENTICE WANTED or BOY NEEDED or HELP WANTED. But, in spite of his efforts to the contrary, Oliver looked so thin and woebegone that when evening came he was still up for sale.

"One boy! Buy a boy!" Mr. Bumble continued to cry. "He's going cheap. Buy a boy."

Some children at play in the street laughed at Oliver, and one of them hit him in the back of the neck with a snowball. Oliver's eyes filled up with tears, but he did his best to smile as Mr. Bumble had commanded.

Just before dusk, a small gaunt man appeared in the doorway of a shop marked SOWERBERRY'S FUNERAL HOME.

14

"How much did you say?" asked the man.

"A mere three pounds, Mr. Sowerberry," cooed Mr. Bumble. "A bargain if there ever was one."

The man beckoned them into the shop. It was a small place full of half-finished coffins and funeral wreaths. Even the dark wooden walls were covered with plans and drawings of coffins.

Over the lid of an unfinished coffin, an evil-looking boy of about eighteen

glared at Oliver. His name was Noah Claypole.

"Missus," called Mr. Sowerberry in a small voice. "Here's Mr. Bumble with a boy for sale."

From the back of the shop Mrs. Sowerberry burst through a curtain and peered sharply at Oliver through weasly eyes. She was short, stout, and beak-nosed. Her dress, like nearly everything else in the shop, was mostly black. Mr. Bumble shifted uneasily, waiting for a decision.

"Too small," said Mrs. Sowerberry at last.

"Maybe so, Mrs. Sowerberry," whee-dled Mr. Bumble. "But he'll grow. I promise you that."

"I daresay he will—on *our* food and *our* drink," she snapped. "Did you really expect us to pay you for the privilege of feeding him? And him too sickly to do a stitch of work? Not likely!"

It looked as if the Sowerberrys were going to turn Oliver away. And though he didn't know what would happen if they did, Oliver was glad to think that he wouldn't be living in such a gloomy place as the funeral shop.

For some time Mr. Sowerberry had been staring at a funeral painting on the wall. Now, suddenly, he spoke up, hum-

16

bly suggesting that Oliver's mournful face might be a perfect addition to funeral processions. Professional mourners were usual, but a child mourner would be extraordinarily touching! Even Mrs. Sowerberry had to agree that her husband's suggestion was a good one.

"Cash on delivery then!" said Mr. Bumble as he held out his hand and began backing toward the door.

"Oh, n-o-o-o, Mr. Bumble!" said Mrs. Sowerberry shrewdly. "Cash upon *liking!* We'll try him out for a week and then decide. Or else you can take him with you right now," she threatened.

It was settled. Oliver would stay on approval. He was to work hard, eat lit-

tle, and march in funeral processions with a high hat on his head and a sad expression on his face.

All this time Noah Claypole had been peering at Oliver and, when no one was looking, making faces at him. He hadn't said anything, but he stared in such a mean way that Oliver felt afraid.

As soon as Mr. Bumble had gone, Mrs. Sowerberry turned to the boy and said, "Noah, you take charge of Oliver. See that he sweeps up, fills the lamps, and earns his keep."

Noah smiled wickedly at Oliver. "I'll take care of him, Missus. Don't you worry about that," he said.

Noah's idea of taking care of Oliver

was to make him as miserable as possible. During the next few days, Oliver tried with all his might to please, but Noah seemed bent on interfering with everything he did. When Oliver swept up a pile of sawdust, Noah walked through it on purpose. When he was filling lamps, Noah bumped into him causing the lamp oil to spill. Oliver, however, said nothing of all this to the Sowerberrys. If he had to be there, he was determined to make the best of things.

When he was not working about the shop, picking up after Noah Claypole, Oliver's sad, thin face could be seen at the head of funeral processions. For this work the Sowerberrys fitted him out with a high silk hat and a black suit, complete with tails. The hat was too big,

but wads of paper kept it from slipping down over his eyes.

This work was easier than the work at the treadmill, but it was also lonelier. And Noah Claypole's mean tricks almost made Oliver wish he were back at the workhouse.

His friends at the workhouse had been a comfort that protected him from the harshness of his life. There had been no boys better or worse off than himself. Now, without them, he found that two new feelings were welling up painfully inside him. For the first time in his life Oliver knew hatred and loneliness. He hated Noah Claypole. And, though he had never known her, he longed for his mother.

Noah somehow sensed that Oliver was yearning for his mother almost at the same moment that Oliver knew it himself. It happened when Oliver was bending over to sweep up some sawdust that Noah had intentionally sprinkled on the floor. Suddenly the bigger boy kicked him sharply from behind.

"How's your mother, workhouse boy?" jeered Noah.

Oliver winced. "You leave her out of it," he said bravely. "She's dead."

"What'sa matter, Workhouse," Noah went on. "Does he miss his Mum?"

It was too much to bear. In a sudden fury, Oliver swung around with his broom and began beating Noah as hard as he could. When the big boy took

19

away the broom, Oliver picked up the huge wooden mallet that was used in the building of coffins.

" 'Elp! 'Elp! Missus Sowerberry!" cried Noah. " 'E's murdering me. The new boy's murdering me!"

Inside and outside the shop, Oliver pursued the cowardly bully. Mrs. Sowerberry rushed out, but Oliver turned on *her* too.

"Hold the brat!" she screamed. "Don't let him go."

Small though he was, it took Noah and Mr. and Mrs. Sowerberry to hold Oliver down. At last they succeeded in shutting him up in one of the coffins. And, while both Sowerberrys sat on the lid of the coffin, Noah ran to fetch Mr. Bumble.

Inside the coffin, Oliver gradually settled down and began to think about his fate. All his life he had done what he had been told to do. And in return he had received nothing but gruel, beatings, hard work, and a board to sleep on. Suddenly he realized that he could stand no more. Though he might starve, he wasn't about to do anything for any Sowerberrys or Claypoles or Bumbles or Corneys any more. Not anything.

20

At the workhouse Mr. Bumble was enjoying the company of Widow Corney when Noah arrived, screaming that the new boy was about to lay siege to the whole town of Dunstable. Mr. Bumble regretted the interruption and he was not happy with the prospect of having Oliver on his hands again. Still he went off with Noah at once, proud to be needed and pleased with the opportunity of lording it over the Sowerberrys.

Brandishing his staff of office, Mr. Bumble entered the Sowerberrys' shop with great bravado. Mr. and Mrs. Sowerberry were still sitting on the coffin lid, which lurched from time to time as Oliver pushed against it with all his might.

"Oliver!" Bumble roared grandly.

"Yes?" said Oliver from inside the coffin.

"You know who this is, Oliver?" asked Bumble.

"Yes."

"And ain't you trembling with fear, Oliver?"

"No, I'm not."

Oliver threw himself against the coffin lid, just as the Sowerberrys leaped off, clutching each other in fear.

"Wa-watch it!" yelped Noah.

"Stand back, everybody," said Mr. Bumble. He waved his heavy staff majestically.

As Oliver emerged stiffly from the coffin, Mr. Bumble grabbed him with one hand, carefully raising his staff in the other. He dragged the struggling but exhausted boy across the floor and shoved him down the basement stairs. From a safe distance, Noah Claypole tossed Oliver's belongings after him.

"We'll see about you in the morning," said Mr. Bumble as he locked the door.

But Oliver had no intentions of waiting for morning. Wandering forlornly about the dark basement in search of a way to escape, he startled a mouse, which scurried up a wall and disappeared. Looking up, Oliver found to his joy that there was a grating over-

head. He piled up some old coffins, climbed on top of them and jiggled the bars. The grating was loose! Quickly he removed it and slipped out into the night, leaving the basement empty of both the mouse and himself.

Just before dawn Oliver managed to slip onto the back of a horse-drawn vegetable wagon. He hid himself in a large bushel of cabbages and waited for several bumpy hours to see where the cart was going. At last the wagon pulled to a halt.

Oliver was just about to peek out of the bushel when the farmer released the catch that allowed the rear of the wagon to tip—spilling cabbages, turnips, and Oliver into the street.

The boy blinked his eyes in the bright morning sun and stared wide-eyed at the sights about him. Flocks of sheep, herds of cattle, and more people than he had ever before seen filled the street —bleating, mooing, and shouting. He was in the rear district of the London market, where farmers came in the early morning to sell their goods to the London shopkeepers.

"Hey you!" cried the farmer as Oliver dazedly scrambled to his feet.

Without waiting to hear what the farmer had to say, Oliver ran through the crowds of people and animals. He

22

plunged down an alley and arrived, breathless but safe, in the midst of a busy street of shops. Slowly he climbed some steps and sat down to rest and think out what he would do next.

He watched hungrily as vendors peddled their wares in the stalls set up on the pavement below him. Then something else caught his eye. A boy, somewhat older than he, was making his way along the pavement. What fascinated Oliver was the manner in which the boy was dressed. He wore a man's overcoat that was so large it nearly reached to his ankles. The coat was open at the front revealing a colorful vest and striped pants as outsized as the coat. To complete the outfit, the boy wore a high silk hat. Only by resting it on his ears did he manage to keep it from slipping over his eyes. The sight was so comical that Oliver would have laughed aloud had the boy not moved so gracefully and casually.

With his hands in his pockets the boy wandered in and around the stalls and barrows, stopping at last beside a fruit stall. There he stood, looking into the air momentarily and whistling to himself. Then, as the fruitseller turned briefly to help a customer, the boy swiftly plucked a couple of plums from the wheelbarrow, whisked them into one of his large pockets, and strolled casually on.

Oliver watched, stunned, as the boy moved to the next stall. Catching sight of Oliver, the boy stared at him steadily for a moment. Then when the lady at the stall was not looking he whipped up a bun from her counter and slipped it, too, into his pocket. He grinned up at Oliver, who looked away, pretending to notice nothing.

Next the boy sat down just a few steps below Oliver and began eating the bun with relish. Oliver watched hungrily as the bun disappeared. The boy looked up.

"Wotcher starin' at?" he said. "Ain't you never seen a lift?"

"I'm sorry," said Oliver.

"It's all right," said the other. "Don't trouble yourself. Hungry?"

"Well, yes," said Oliver slowly. "It *has* been a while——"

"Catch," said the boy.

He tossed Oliver one of the plums and watched, pleased, as Oliver stuffed the whole thing into his mouth at once.

"Running away from the beak?" said the bigger boy.

"The what?" said Oliver.

"The beak. Don't say you don't know what a beak is?"

"It's a bird's mouth, isn't it?" said Oliver.

"I say, you *are* green!" laughed the older boy. "A beak's a constable! A policeman! Who are you running from then—your old man? Are you running away from home?"

"No, I'm an orphan," said Oliver. "I've come to London to seek my fortune."

The boy moved up next to Oliver and looked at him with interest.

"Oh you have, have you?" he said confidentially. "Got any lodgin's?"

Oliver shook his head.

"I see," said the boy thoughtfully. "Then you'll be needing a place to stay tonight, eh?"

"Do you know of one?" asked Oliver.

"I might do, matie," said the boy. "I

might do. I know a respectable gentleman what'll give you lodgin's for nothing if you've got a proper introduction. And I can take care of that—that is, if you'll tell me your name."

"It's Oliver. Oliver Twist."

"And mine's Jack Dawkins," said the boy cheerfully. "Better known among me friends as the Artful Dodger."

"What does that mean?" Oliver asked.

The Dodger looked at him mysteriously for a moment, then put his arm around Oliver and led him down the steps.

"You'll find out soon enough," he said. "Come on now and welcome to London. Consider yourself at 'ome!"

Skipping and darting about, the Dodger maneuvered deftly through the better districts of London. At first

27

Oliver was bewildered and uncertain. But the merriment was catching and, soon, he too was laughing gaily and frisking about the streets like his new friend.

" 'Ome" as the Dodger called it, was located in the worst part of London. Oliver followed his friend down scary dark alleys, where beggars tried to sleep, up wooden stairs that shook with age, and across rooftops of rat-infested tenements. At last, after crossing a footbridge between two buildings, the Dodger opened a rooftop door and pulled Oliver in after him.

The room in which Oliver found himself was a sort of attic or loft. Like the rest of the neighborhood, it was dilapidated and run-down. Light filtered through a filthy skylight in the roof, revealing dingy wooden walls and a sagging plank floor. Across the room a wide chimney had been broken open to serve as a sort of kitchen. The crevice in the chimney was wide, and the bricks removed from it had been carefully piled in one corner, making a small fireplace within the chimney. Clouds of steam billowed energetically from a large kettle above the fire. In another corner of the chimney kitchen hung an assortment of pots, pans, and long forks.

But Oliver scarcely noticed all this. Instead, he stared in astonishment and delight at something else in the room. Lounging about on sacking beds or dangling their feet from the rafters were more than a dozen boys of about his own age or older. They gazed at Oliver with silent interest.

"Evenin' all," said the Dodger. "Where's Fagin?"

A tall, skinny old man peered out of the chimney kitchen. He had a straggly beard and long wild hair, and he wore a long flannel robe that hung loosely about him. His face lit up with pleasure as he saw the Dodger. Oliver sensed that the two must be special friends.

"Here, I am, Dodger, my dear," said Fagin.

"I've brought a new lodger—name's Oliver," said the Dodger. "Oliver Twist."

The Dodger pushed Oliver forward toward Fagin, who looked at him out of sharp but kindly eyes. The old man bowed ridiculously and offered his bony hand for Oliver to shake.

"How do you do, my dear," he said.

"H-how do you do, sir?" said Oliver.

"I hope you'll feel very welcome here, Oliver," said Fagin with a mischievous twinkle in his eyes. "We're very glad

to see you, aren't we, my dears?"

At this the boys sprang to life. Dropping from rafters and leaping from corners, they crowded around Oliver.

" 'Course we are! How are you, Oliver. Welcome!" they chattered.

Fagin whispered quietly with the Dodger and then turned again to the boys, flapping among them like a mad hen. "Now, get cracking," he ordered. "You there, mind the sausages."

Oliver sat down quietly on a packing case and looked about the loft. Someone tossed him a sausage, which he gulped down with relish. The room was a shambles, very unlike the workhouse, which the orphan boys had been forced to keep spotlessly clean. But it was warm and friendly, also unlike the workhouse, and Oliver liked it. The only truly unpleasant thing Oliver noticed was a mean-looking man who sat scowling in a chair near a window. The boys addressed him as Bill or Mr. Sikes, but whenever possible they avoided him altogether. Oliver thought to himself that he, too, would try to stay clear of Bill Sikes.

He went on with his survey of the loft, gazing up at the rafters. Between them were stretched yards and yards of string and twine from which hung hundreds of pocket handkerchiefs. Oliver looked at these curiously.

"Is this a laundry, then, sir?" he asked as Fagin sat down beside him.

The boys laughed.

"Not exactly," chuckled Fagin. "We've a better line of business haven't we, boys?"

"I should say so—and how!" came the replies as the boys laughed again.

"Come then, my dears," said Fagin. "Let's show Oliver how we do it. You see, Oliver," he went on, "there's one thing in life that counts—and that's

money in the bank. Am I right, boys?"

The boys cheered as Fagin strode over to a chest in a corner of the loft. From it he took out two or three handkerchiefs, a wallet, a watch and chain, a spectacle case, and a snuff box. All of these he stuffed into the numerous pockets of his tremendous robe. Then he began strutting about like a proper gentleman.

"Lovely day, ain't it?" he said to one boy. "And the top of the morning to you, kind sir." He tipped his hat to imaginary passers-by and pretended to look into a store window.

Winking to each other the boys, too, began bustling about, pretending to ignore Fagin altogether. They walked past him as if in a crowd, and one boy accidentally pushed another into him.

As the pretense went on, a box became a park bench on which Fagin sat to enjoy a view of the imaginary park. Two boys promptly sat down on either side of him and, while one pretended to converse with Fagin, the other whistled and looked away.

Oliver watched all of this closely, wondering if it was a game or a play. If it was a game, what could the point of it be? He was fascinated, but completely mystified.

"All right, lads," said Fagin at last. "The game's over. Let's see how you've managed."

He called all the boys, including Oliver, to a table in the center of the room. Very dramatically he turned each of his many pockets inside out. To Oliver's amazement, they were all entirely empty!

Then one by one the boys produced the handkerchiefs, wallet, watch, snuff box, and spectacle case. They held them up proudly before Oliver's admiring eyes. So that was the game! The boys had taken everything from Fagin's pocket without his or Oliver's noticing at all! Oliver wondered how they had done it—and why.

After everything had been returned to the chest, Fagin held a sort of council.

"Now, then," he said. "I hope you've

all been hard at work today, my dears?"

" 'Course we have," shouted a boy.

"Good boys—good boys," said Fagin with a twinkle. "Now, Dodger, what have you got to show?"

The Artful Dodger stepped forward and presented Fagin with two wallets. Fagin, in turn, offered them to Oliver for his inspection.

"Nicely made, wouldn't you say, Oliver?"

Oliver studied the wallets. "Yes, sir," he said. "Did the Dodger really make them himself?"

He was looking so intently at Fagin that he didn't see the boys nudge each other in amusement.

"In a manner of speaking," said Fagin. "And you'd like to learn to make wallets like that wouldn't you, my dear?"

"Oh, yes, sir!" said Oliver.

Another boy turned in a couple of handkerchiefs with fancy initials in the corners.

"Very nice, my dear," said Fagin. "But you've not done well with the initials. I'm afraid they'll have to be picked out. Oliver," he said, "you'll have to learn to do that, too, won't you, my dear?"

"Yes, sir," said Oliver, "if you'll teach me how."

This time the boys could not hide their laughter. Oliver looked at them in bewilderment, but Fagin put up a hand for silence.

"Of course, I'll teach you, my dear," he said to Oliver. "And so will the Dodger. You do just as he does."

Fagin ruffled the Dodger's hair affectionately.

"But now let's have another little game," he said. "Are you ready for your first lesson?"

Oliver watched eagerly as Fagin walked toward the fireplace. He did something with his hands which Oliver could not see. Then suddenly he spun around and peered intently at Oliver.

"Tell me, my dear," he said. "Is my handkerchief protruding from my pocket?"

Oliver looked closely. "Yes, sir," he said. "I can just see the corner."

"Very good, my dear!" said Fagin. "Now, see if you can take it out without my feeling anything—just as you saw the others do."

Once again Fagin began strutting about the room, humming to himself. Oliver followed. He got nearer and nearer to Fagin. It didn't seem hard. In fact, he thought it ought to be very easy. He reached out his hand toward the pocket. But just when he thought he

33

could grasp the handkerchief, Fagin spun around so that the pocket was out of reach. The boys snickered, but Oliver tried again. Over and over he stole close to the handkerchief. But every time he thought he had Fagin fooled, the old man turned and Oliver had to begin again. The more he tried, the more the boys laughed. Oliver began to feel foolish. He was just about to give up when, for the first time, Fagin failed to turn. As gently as he could, Oliver plucked the handkerchief away. It was almost too easy and Oliver wondered if Fagin had intentionally let him succeed. But the old man wiped away his doubts.

"Is it gone?" he said with apparent astonishment.

"Yes, sir!" said Oliver triumphantly. He held up the handkerchief proudly.

"Well, fancy that!" said Fagin, patting Oliver on the head. "You're a clever boy, my dear—never saw a sharper lad."

There was much grumbling and protesting as Fagin herded the boys off to their beds on the floor. But Oliver could see that all of the boys loved the odd old man.

"Where shall *I* sleep, sir?" he asked at last.

Fagin led Oliver to a corner near the fireplace. With a flourish he arranged some sacks in a kind of broken basket, clowning as though he were making up a real bed.

"A nice cozy bed by the fire," he said. "You'll be lovely and warm here and

tomorrow we'll play some more games, eh?"

"Yes, sir. Thank you, sir," said Oliver.

"Sweet dreams, my dear," said Fagin. "Sweet dreams."

From his sacking bed, Oliver watched as Fagin crept about the room. He blew out all of the candles but one. Then, humming a peculiar lullaby about money, he slipped out the door. He was a strange old man, Oliver thought. Indeed, nearly everything about his new home seemed strange. There was something almost mysterious about it. But at the same time it was friendly and welcoming and Oliver liked it. He felt happier than he had ever been in his life.

Oliver slept, peacefully dreaming of nothing, until sometime late in the night, when the sound of Fagin's chuckling woke him. He watched silently as the old man placed a candle on the table and crept over to the fireplace near Oliver's bed. Kneeling down he raised a loose floorboard and removed a large wooden box bound sturdily with metal

bands. Oliver could tell that the chest was heavy as he watched Fagin lug it back to the candlelit table.

The old man sat down at the table and, after peering cautiously about the room, raised the lid of the box. Out of it he lifted a huge gold watch and chain, which he proceeded to swing back and forth in front of his face.

"Tick tock, lovely watch," he cooed. His eyes moved back and forth, following the watch as if he had been hypnotized.

What Oliver saw next made his eyes grow wide with wonder. Suddenly Fagin plunged his hands into the box and began sifting piles of diamond, pearl, and emerald jewelry through his long fingers.

"And it's mine—all mine!" he said. "Nobody can take my secret treasure from me. It will keep me when I'm old. After all, somebody's got to look after me, haven't they?"

He looked about the dark room full of sleeping boys. "Will *you?*" he whispered. "Will *you* look after your old Fagin?"

Suddenly his eyes fell on Oliver, who

had propped himself up on one elbow and was staring at the old man in amazement. Fagin slammed down the lid of the chest, jumped to his feet, and hurried over to the boy.

Terrified by the angry look on Fagin's face, Oliver sat up.

"You're awake!" said Fagin in a sharp voice. "Why are you watching me? What did you see? Quick now," he demanded, "what did you see?"

"I'm sorry if I disturbed you, sir." said Oliver nervously.

"Were you awake when I fetched my little box?"

"No, sir," said Oliver, not daring to speak the truth.

"Are you sure?"

"Yes, sir. Quite sure."

Slowly Fagin seemed to relax. He patted Oliver gently on the head.

"Ah, yes," he said. "I knew that all along, my dear."

He rubbed his hands together, chuckling and looking uneasily at the table. Crossing to it, he placed his hand on the box and questioned Oliver again.

"Did you see any of the pretty things in this, my dear?" he asked.

Seeing that Fagin was calm once more, Oliver spoke up honestly.

"Yes, sir!" he said.

"Well, they're mine!" Fagin hissed fiercely. "It's all I have to live on in my old age!"

He returned to Oliver and whispered confidentially.

"Some people say I'm a miser," he said. "But it's a terrible thing, old age, Oliver. And I'll need my secret treasure then."

Oliver did not understand the strange old man at all.

"Can I go to sleep again, sir?" he asked.

"Yes, that's right," said Fagin soothingly. "You go to sleep. Old Fagin won't disturb you again. Sleep, now—it's all been a dream."

Once more Oliver closed his eyes and pretended to sleep. But his brain was wide awake. He was nearly frantic with fright and confusion. So much had happened that he could not understand. He thought about the Dodger stealing plums and buns and hiding them in his gigantic coat. He thought of the handkerchiefs hanging about the room, and of the peculiar pocket-picking game he had learned earlier. And what of Fagin? Fagin was the greatest mystery of all— so kind one minute, and in such a rage the next. This place was not a workhouse and yet it was not possible for Fagin to be the father of all of the boys. Why then had this strange, shabby man

38

taken in so many boys? Why did he want Oliver? And was he rich? There was something about it all that seemed dishonest and disturbing to Oliver. But he thought again of the welcome he had received—the food and the friendliness —and, gradually, he went back to sleep.

In the morning Oliver woke to his new home and his first hot breakfast. Seated at the table, he gratefully shared a seemingly unlimited supply of toast, sausages, and steaming coffee with the other boys. It was the best breakfast he had ever eaten and, with good food before him, he was finding it easy to forget the mysterious events of the previous night.

A shout of joy went up when a pretty lady called Nancy entered with a younger girl and began passing out

sweet rolls. At first it seemed to Oliver that the boys, by clowning and cracking jokes, were treating her disrespectfully. But he soon saw that the teasing was full of admiration and that the kind woman loved it. Her affectionate nature made everyone feel carefree and Oliver thought Nancy was the most likable person he had ever known.

After breakfast, he watched admiringly as the boys prepared to leave for what they called their "work." He thought of the beautiful wallets that the Dodger had produced the day before, and he was eager to learn to make them as Fagin had promised he could. Walk-ing over to the Dodger, he asked humbly if he could please go along.

"Hey, Fagin!" said the Dodger. "Young Oliver wants to work with us today."

"Eh? What's that?" said the old man. "On the job, you mean?"

"May I, sir?" pleaded Oliver. "I'd like to help."

He waited anxiously for the answer.

"Yes, you can go," said Fagin after a pause. "Good luck on your first job, my dear. Make lots of wallets and hand-kerchiefs and I'll be waiting for you when you come back."

In his excitement, Oliver was unaware of the other boys' amusement. Thrilled to be a part of things, he followed them out the door. They crossed the rooftop bridge and thundered down the stairs to the street, where they split up into small groups of twos and threes. Oliver was to go with the Dodger and a boy named Charlie Bates, but he hesitated a moment in order to wave goodby to Fagin, who was now standing on the bridge. The old man waved back affectionately and Oliver, brimming with happiness, hurried after his new friends.

It was still early as Oliver, the Dodger, and Charlie Bates sauntered through the back alleys of London on their way to work. But already the streets were crowded with workers, hurrying to and fro in a frenzy of money-making activity. The doors of warehouses were flung open, allowing much business to be carried on in the streets and alleys. Butchers in bloody aprons chopped away at huge sides of beef. Newspaper boys waving the morning paper charged about in frantic competition with each other. Buttermaids churned, chimney sweepers swept, and bottle washers washed. To Oliver it all seemed a sort of wonderful dance. Everyone had somewhere to go and something to do. And Oliver was grateful that he, too, had a purpose to carry out.

For a while the boys stood and

watched a street circus. Accompanied by the *oom-boop-boop* of a half-empty carousel, two acrobats tossed each other about skillfully. Oliver clenched his fists in sympathy as a gigantic man grunted and raised an enormous dumbbell. He gasped as the man with a beard tipped back his head and swallowed the flames of a blazing torch, while still another opened his throat to receive the entire blade of a two-foot-long sword.

A horse-drawn omnibus clattered past and, following the example of the Dodger and Charlie, Oliver mounted the back for a free ride. For a while they clung undetected to the back of the bus, but then a stuffy passenger poked at them with an umbrella and they had to flee.

It was nearly noon when the three boys found themselves in a wealthy section of London called Clerkenwell. The

mood here was different and more gracious as fine ladies and gentlemen paraded in and out of shops, greeting each other with much raising of hats, bowing, and curtseying.

Oliver followed the Dodger and Charlie down the street, sticking his hands in his pockets and trying to appear as casual and unimpressed as they did. But he did not feel casual in the least. Drapery, bakery, grocery and china shops lined the street, their windows full of beautiful and delicious goods such as Oliver had never imagined.

The three boys lingered hungrily before the bakery window. Inside, an enormous woman stared haughtily back as if daring the urchin trio to enter. Oliver was shocked when his two companions mimicked her expression disrespectfully

43

and went off laughing. But, hanging back at the window, he was struck by their perfect imitation of the woman. He giggled and hurried after his friends.

He found them standing in the doorway of a shop, carefully watching something across the street.

"How 'bout it, Charlie?" asked the Dodger.

Oliver followed their gaze. Across the street was a bookshop and in front of it, studying a book from an outside display case, stood a tall, gray-haired gentleman in fancy clothes. He wore a gray top hat, a green coat with a black-velvet collar, and tailored white trousers.

"Well, Charlie?" asked the Dodger again.

"He'll do," said Charlie with a nod. The two boys sauntered across the

44

street. After a moment's hesitation, Oliver followed, watching closely, a puzzled expression on his face. The Dodger and Charlie stopped on the other side of the street just a few yards from the bookshop. They winked significantly at each other and then strolled along the pavement until they stood directly behind the elderly gentleman. The man continued reading while, much to Oliver's horror, the Dodger raised the green coattail and swiftly removed the wallet from the man's hip pocket.

Feeling the movement of his coattail, the man looked up from his book and put a hand to his pocket. It was only as the man himself discovered his wallet was missing that Oliver fully understood what was happening. In one terrible split second everything became clear to him. The wallets that Oliver thought the Dodger had made were stolen, just like the plums and bun from the market. The handkerchiefs, too, had been stolen and the initials were to be picked out so that Fagin could sell them as new ones. All of Fagin's boys were pickpockets! And the silver and jewels and all the other valuable things that Fagin kept in his secret box—these, too, had surely been stolen! Utterly horrified, Oliver realized that he, too, was expected to steal!

He stood stunned for a moment as he tried to take all of this in. Then, looking up, he suddenly became aware that the Dodger and Charlie had disappeared. The man in the green coat spun around just as Oliver gathered his wits and began to run.

"Stop! Stop, thief!" called the man, pointing at Oliver.

At once several other gentlemen took up the cry and a dozen or so others began chasing the frightened boy.

In complete panic, Oliver struggled through the crowd, dodging the many hands that reached out to block his way. As he ran past an alley he caught sight of the Dodger and Charlie. With a sense of relief he started toward them. They would help, he was sure. But just then Charlie, too, cried, "Stop thief!" and

the two boys sprang out of the alley toward Oliver.

His heart sank at this betrayal, but once, when he stumbled over a cobblestone, he saw the Dodger bend to tie his shoe, causing several men to trip and fall. Oliver understood. They *were* trying to help, but there was no sense in all three of them being caught. Over his shoulder he saw Charlie trying to mislead the crowd by yelling "Stop, thief!" again and running off in the wrong direction.

But all efforts to help were useless. The boys managed to mislead a few men, but the main body of Oliver's pursuers remained close behind him. Ahead, more stood ready to take up the chase when others tired.

Then, suddenly, Oliver thought he saw a way to escape. He ducked quickly into a shopping arcade. Panting and gasping for air, he huddled in a doorway and looked back toward the street. His pursuers ran by, unaware that their quarry was not ahead somewhere in the crowd. He had fooled them! But Oliver knew he was not safe yet. In a moment they would discover their error and be back, looking for him in the arcade. Frantically, Oliver searched for a new escape route.

He spotted an alley that connected

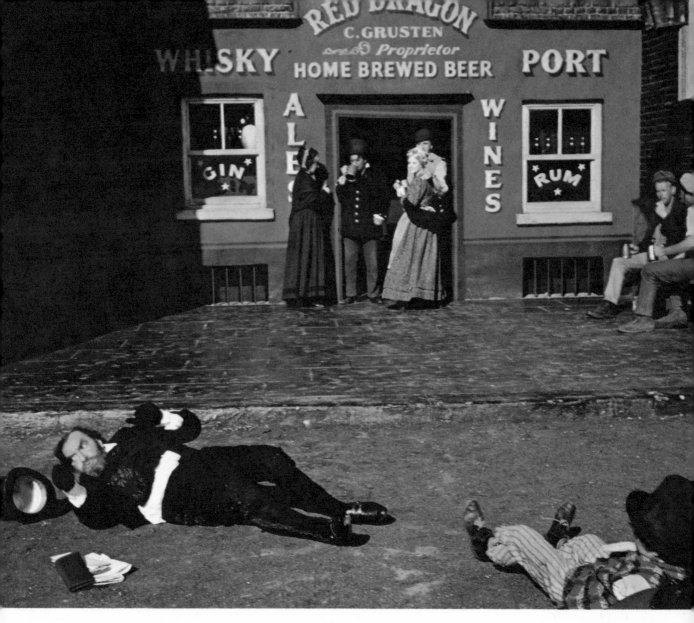

the arcade with another street! If he could just get through it before the crowd discovered him, he would lose himself in a different throng of shoppers. So far no one was behind him. In a moment he would be safe.

Glancing over his shoulder, Oliver saw with relief that there was still no one following. Now at last he could relax—but not for long. Nearly overcome with exhaustion, he stumbled down the last few steps only to find that he had run a circle and was back in front of the bookshop. Standing there, talking excitedly with a constable, was the gentleman in the green coat! Before Oliver could turn, the man looked up and shouted, "There he is! That's the boy!"

Unable to run another step, Oliver was quickly pinned to the ground by a

hefty workman. Angry-faced ladies and gentlemen bent over him accusingly. He did not struggle as the constable pulled him to his feet and presented him to the man in the green coat.

"Is this the thief, Mr. Brownlow?" asked the constable. "Do you identify this boy as the one who stole your wallet?"

"Well," said Mr. Brownlow. "He *is* the boy I saw running away, and——"

"That's enough for me," interrupted the constable. "Come on young feller, let's see how you like spending the night in the lock-up. And tomorrow," he added, "we'll have you up in court before the magistrate."

As the constable dragged him away,

Oliver caught sight of the Dodger and Charlie Bates milling about in the dwindling crowd. But he said nothing to the constable about them. They had been good to him and had tried to help. He wouldn't say anything to anyone about what he had seen.

As the constable had promised, Oliver was indeed taken into court the next morning. There he was placed in the dock, a sort of wooden pen guarded by two constables. A dozen or so onlookers sat behind a wooden barrier at the back of the courtroom.

The magistrate, a skinny, bad-tempered man, entered and took his place at the front of the court. Peering nearsightedly over his glasses, he signaled to

a clerk, who brought Mr. Brownlow to the magistrate's desk.

"And what crime is this fellow charged with?" demanded the magistrate. "He looks a perfect scoundrel."

Mr. Brownlow looked outraged.

"He's not charged at all, your worship," said the clerk. "This gentleman, Mr. Brownlow, is the plaintiff. He is appearing against the boy."

Laughter rippled through the courtroom.

"Boy?" snapped the magistrate. "What boy?"

"The boy in the dock, your worship," said the clerk.

"Well, stand up, boy!" said the magistrate. "I can't see you!"

"He *is* standing, your worship," said the constable.

Again the court laughed. Ten minutes passed and still the magistrate was unable to find out who was on trial and for what. He called upon one person after another, impatiently interrupting each one and then misinterpreting what had been said. Mr. Brownlow grew angrier and angrier at the magistrate's impossible behavior.

"What are we waiting for?" shouted the magistrate at last. "Brownly, or whatever your name is, *will* you state your complaint against this boy or not?"

Carefully controlling his temper, Mr. Brownlow began to speak softly. "My name, sir, is Brownlow," he said. "Yesterday afternoon I was standing at a bookstall when——"

"Yes, yes," said the magistrate. "Never mind that."

He turned to Oliver, who stood in the dock, pale with fear and lack of sleep.

"What's your name, boy?" he asked.

"Oliver," said Oliver in a small whisper.

"I can't *hear* you!" bellowed the magistrate.

The constable at the dock bent down and listened to Oliver.

"He says his name is Oliver Twist, sir," he reported.

The constable continued to relay Oliver's whispered answers to the magistrate. No, the boy had no parents. Yes, he was an orphan.

The magistrate inquired as to where Oliver lived.

"He don't seem to be able to say where he lives, nor anything else, sir," reported the constable.

"Well," said the magistrate. "He's a liar and a thief and an insolent beggar as well. The boy is committed to prison for three months' hard labor. Clear the court!"

Unable to control his anger any

longer, Mr. Brownlow thumped his walking stick on the courtroom floor.

"Upon my soul!" he cried. "This is disgraceful. I demand to be heard."

But just then a man burst into the court announcing that his name was Jessop and that he was the owner of the bookstore where the crime had supposedly occurred.

"Wait!" he cried. "Don't take the boy away!"

"Clear the court!" repeated the magistrate.

"No!" shouted Jessop. "I saw what happened. Two other boys stole Mr. Brownlow's wallet. This boy had nothing to do with it."

He explained that he had only just heard about the trial and had rushed right over. In spite of the magistrate's protestations, he continued to explain that Mr. Brownlow had been reading a book outside his shop when——

"Book?" interrupted the magistrate. "What book? Has he paid for it."

Mr. Jessop grinned. "Not yet," he said, "but I know Mr. Brownlow well——"

"Dear me!" said Mr. Brownlow. "I forgot all about it!"

"Ah ha!" cried the magistrate. "A fine fellow you are to accuse a poor innocent orphan. Forgot to pay, indeed!"

Mr. Brownlow opened his mouth to protest, but the magistrate would hear no more. "Hold your tongue!" he said. "The boy is discharged. Clear the court!"

In utter disgust Mr. Brownlow stamped his foot and cracked his walking stick in two over his knee.

Outside the court a carriage drawn by two horses stood waiting at the curb. Oliver came slowly through the courtroom door, looking dazed and bewildered. Where would he go now, he wondered. Should he go back to Fagin's? And if he did, how would he find his way? And if he found his way, would he then have to become a thief?

Mr. Brownlow, still spluttering, came hurrying out with Mr. Jessop. He rushed over to Oliver.

"My poor boy," he said. "I can never forgive myself for my stupidity."

"It was my fault for running away, sir," said Oliver.

But Mr. Brownlow was determined to make amends. He bade good-by to Mr. Jessop, promising to pay for the book shortly. Then, putting his arm around Oliver, he led him to the horse-drawn carriage at the curb.

"Come now," he said cheerfully. "In you get!"

"But, sir," said Oliver. "Where are we going?"

"Home," said the gentleman.

The next morning the sun shone brightly again. And Bloomsbury Square, far from Fagin's den, fairly glistened. The square was an elegant green park, rich with trees and sweet-scented flowers. Around it ran a wide, clean cobblestone street which was lined with fine houses—formal, white, and expensive-looking. As the sun warmed the square, birds in the green trees chirped cheerfully. And slowly, from the dingy back alleys of poorer London, the shabby street vendors began to emerge, blending their plaintive songs with the cheerful ones of the birds, and gently rousing the wealthy ladies and gentlemen who lived around Bloomsbury Square.

The first vendor to arrive was a pretty flower girl.

"Who will buy my sweet red roses?" she piped. Reaching into her flat basket, she waved several crimson buds toward the sparkling windows.

More and more vendors began to appear—a milkmaid with two buckets hanging from a yoke across her shoulders, and a strawberry vendor, a plump jolly woman with cheeks to match her wares. Their cries mingled musically with the song of the flower girl.

Then came the onion man, the costermongers, errand boys, and the knife grinder. And slowly the houses, too, seemed to wake to the day as maids and stewards hurried to receive provisions, barter over prices, sweep mats, or shake mops out of windows.

At last the finely clad ladies and gentlemen of the square were lured out to take the air, swinging canes and twirling parasols to protect white skin from the bright sun.

And someone else was stirred from sleep by the sounds of the morning. In one of the fine houses facing the square, Oliver Twist awoke to find himself in a soft, striped nightgown, tucked cozily in a tremendous, soft bed. Never before had he slept in a real bed and he found the luxurious comfort of clean, white

sheets and feather quilts so astonishing that, for a moment, he could not remember where he was. Even his hair was soft and clean! Then, looking about the carpeted room, he remembered coming in a horse-drawn carriage with Mr. Brownlow, whose merry, stout house-keeper, Mrs. Bedwin, had fed and bathed him and tucked him into bed.

Across the room, lace curtains drifted before an open French door. Hearing the lovely cries of the vendors, Oliver climbed out of bed and rushed out onto the balcony. By this time, the early risers had been joined by others. On the green, school children paused to romp by a clear pond and prim nurses in white stockings paraded fancy baby carriages. To Oliver, it all seemed a wonderful dream. With the music of the vendors in his ears and the warm sun on his face, he wanted to join in the singing. He did not know exactly what lay ahead of him. There might well be more troubles. But somehow, with this glorious, beautiful, wonderful morning before him, Oliver felt certain that his life would turn out to be a happy one.

The blue sky, the brightly dressed people and wares—it was almost enough just to have had a chance to see this remarkable, happy world.